For Caroline —J.S.
For my parents   P.P.

Text copyright © 1998 by James Sage
Illustrations copyright © 1998 by Pierre Pratt
All rights reserved.
Published in the United States 1998
by Dutton Children's Books,
a member of Penguin Putnam Inc.
375 Hudson Street, New York, New York 10014
Originally published in Great Britain 1998
by Macmillan Children's Books, London
Typography by Ellen M. Lucaire
Printed in Belgium
First American Edition
ISBN 0-525-45885-9
2 4 6 8 10 9 7 5 3 1

Sassy Gracie

by James Sage
illustrated by Pierre Pratt

Dutton Children's Books New York

Sassy Gracie had a pair of big red shoes with big red heels that she loved to pieces.

When she went prancing about in them—which Cook said was far too often—they sounded like this:

CLUNKETY-CLUNK! CLUNKETY-CLUNK!

Stop that dancing, Sassy Gracie!
It's getting on my nerves!

Now one day, which happened to be Cook's day off, the master of the big house came to see Sassy Gracie in the kitchen. He walked with a big stick, which sounded like this:
BUMPETY-BUMP! BUMPETY-BUMP! BUMPETY-BUMP!

Sassy Gracie, I'm expecting a very important guest for dinner. Two roast chickens will do nicely.

So Sassy Gracie hurried off to market **CLUNKETY-CLUNK!**
CLUNKETY-CLUNK! and bought two of the plumpest little
chickens she could find.

Then she hurried back to the big house.

Well, there wasn't much to do while the chickens were roasting, except kick up her heels by the stove. And the more Sassy Gracie kicked up her big red heels, the more she felt like dancing.

Cook not being here to stop me, you know!

So she did.

She danced all around the kitchen **CLUNKETY-CLUNK!**
down the hall **CLUNKETY-CLUNK!**
around the best sitting room **CLUNKETY-CLUNK!**
through the dining room **CLUNKETY-CLUNK!**
in and out of the master's library . . .

. . . and back to the kitchen.

Whew! Dancing sure can wear you out!

Now, by this time, the chickens had cooked to a perfect golden brown, but the guest still had not appeared.

Sassy Gracie went to see the master.

*If that guest of yours doesn't show up soon,
my chickens will be ruined!*

So the master sent the stableboy to look for the guest. Sassy Gracie went **CLUNKETY-CLUNK!** back to the kitchen and took the chickens out of the oven.

As the chickens sat there cooling, Sassy Gracie began to wonder if they really were cooked through. So, she thought she had better take a little nibble of one.

Well, the wing's okay,
but who knows about that drumstick?

She had another little nibble . . .

Just to make sure!

And another . . . and another . . . until the chicken was no more than a spiky carcass of well-picked bones!

Eating all that chicken made her feel so frisky that
she started dancing all over again . . .
out the back door **CLUNKETY-CLUNK!**
into Cook's kitchen garden **CLUNKETY-CLUNK!**
through the stable yard **CLUNKETY-CLUNK!**
over the bridge **CLUNKETY-CLUNK!**
across the meadow . . .

. . . and back to the kitchen, where she noticed the second chicken still cooling on the table. And she began to wonder if it could possibly be as well-cooked as the first.

Well, there is only one way to find out,
and that's to taste it. After all, every cook
is allowed a nibble now and then!

And soon the second chicken was no more than a spiky carcass of well-picked bones, just like the first.

My oh my! That sure was tasty,
if I do say so myself.

And then she heard the master call.

Sassy Gracie! Sassy Gracie!
My guest is arriving! Get the dinner ready!

Oh no! What was Sassy Gracie going to do now? She had eaten both chickens!

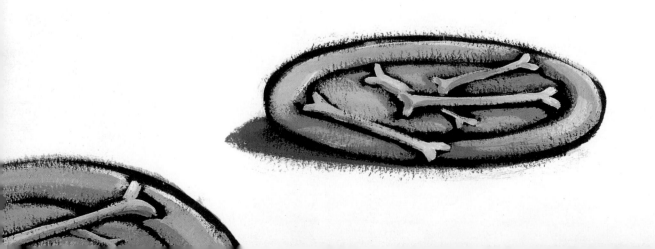

Well, this is what she did. She scooted out the back door and around the house to the front **CLUNKETY-CLUNK! CLUNKETY-CLUNK!** where she bumped into the guest coming up the walk.

Mister, are you ever in trouble!
If I were you, I'd hotfoot it home while the going is good.
Because you're so late, my master is planning to give you
two big bumps on your head with his walking stick!
Listen, you can hear him coming now!

The guest listened, and sure enough, this is what he heard:

BUMPETY-BUMP!

BUMPETY-BUMP!

BUMPETY-BUMP!

So, naturally, he took off running in the opposite direction . . .
while Sassy Gracie scooted back into the house **CLUNKETY-CLUNK!**
to speak to the master.

That's a fine guest you invited!
He's run off with my two roast chickens!

The master was very annoyed.

You don't say! Both roast chickens? A fine guest, indeed!
He might at least have left me one to eat!

And away he ran, waving his walking stick in the air and shouting:

Stop! Only one! All I want is one!

But the poor guest—thinking his host now meant to give him one
big bump on the head instead of two—ran all the faster.

And Sassy Gracie?
Well, she went
prancing up the stairs
CLUNKETY-CLUNK!

to her little room at
the top of the house
CLUNKETY-CLUNK!

and plopped herself
on her big brass bed
CLUNK!

where she kicked off
one big red shoe
with its big red heel
CLUNK!

and the other big red shoe
with its big red heel
CLUNK!

and before she knew it,
she was fast asleep.
And did she snore,
having danced all day and
eaten so much chicken?

YOU BET SHE DID!